First published in Great Britain in 1999 by Madcap Books,
André Deutsch Ltd,
76 Dean Street,
London, W1V 5HA
www.vci.co.uk

Concept and text copyright © Madcap Books/Gyles Brandreth
Illustrations copyright © 1999 Peter Dennis

A catalogue record for this title is available from the British Library

ISBN 0 233 99533 1

Designed by Design 23

Printed in Belgium

BRUNO BRUIN DISCOVERS AMERICA

Gyles Brandreth

Illustrations by

Peter Dennis

MADCAP

In days of old, when knights were bold, the boldest and the bravest of them all was Sir Bruno Bruin.

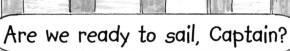

A desert island!

But, it's not on the map!

You've discovered it, Boss. You can call it Bruin Island. You'll be famous.

I already am, aren't I?

It looks beautiful, Boss. I bet there are delicious things to eat on that island.

Let's go see!

Ta-da!

How do you do?

Bloo-bloop.

I can't swim.

But I can float!

This is my kind of desert island, Boss.

Except it isn't deserted, Rocco.

Look!

Sh! Follow me.

Sh! Follow me.

Right, we'll camp here tonight and set off in the morning.

What's for supper, Boss?

Stinging nettle soup.

My favourite.

My hero!

Gurgle.

What was that?

SWOOSH!

We're being attacked by Indians!